Sigmund B...

Watch Out for Joel!

Mystery Pennies

BETHANY BACKYARD®

www.bethanyhouse.com

Mystery Pennies
Copyright © 2003
Sigmund Brouwer

Cover and interior illustrations by Tammie Lyon/Laurie Lambert Association
Cover design by Jennifer Parker

Unless otherwise identified, Scripture quotations are from the *International Children's Bible, New Century Version,* copyright © 1986, 1988 by Word Publishing, Dallas, Texas 75039. Used by permission.

Published by Bethany House Publishers
11400 Hampshire Avenue South
Bloomington, Minnesota 55438
www.bethanyhouse.com

Bethany House Publishers is a Division of
Baker Book House Company, Grand Rapids, Michigan.

Printed in China

Library of Congress Cataloging-in-Publication Data

CIP data applied for

ISBN 0-7642-2584-7

Brotherly Love

Ricky tricks Joel with mystery pennies to get Joel to do his work. How will Ricky's dishonesty make him feel?

Romans 18:9 says, "Your love must be real. Hate what is evil. Hold on to what is good." Ricky needs to learn about loving his brother and treating him fairly. As you read the story, can you think of a time when you acted like Ricky?

1

"Can I help you deliver newspapers today?" Joel asked his brother, Ricky.

"No," Ricky said to his brother, Joel. "I am thirteen. You are seven. I don't need your help. Not today. Not ever. Do you understand?"

"Yes," Joel said. "I understand."

Ricky walked away with the newspapers to deliver. Every day, Ricky delivered newspapers to forty houses. He got paid one dime for each house. That meant he made four dollars every day for delivering newspapers.

Joel watched Ricky walk away to deliver newspapers.

Joel followed. But Joel stayed hidden from his older brother, Ricky.

Soon, Joel saw Ricky pull out a water pistol from his pocket.

Joel wanted to ask why Ricky needed a water pistol to deliver newspapers. But Joel stayed hidden from his older brother.

2

Then Joel saw why Ricky needed a water pistol.

When Ricky passed by a house with two big dogs behind a fence, Ricky squirted the dogs with water.

It made the dogs mad. The dogs barked and barked.

Ricky laughed at the dogs.

Ricky did not see Joel come up from behind.

Joel tapped Ricky on the shoulder.

It scared Ricky.

Ricky jumped.

When Ricky landed, Joel asked him a question.

"Why are you mean to the dogs?" Joel asked.

"The dogs always bark at me," Ricky said. "So I squirt them with water."

"They bark at you because you squirt them first," Joel said.

"What do you know?" Ricky asked. "You are only seven. And I told you I did not need your help to deliver the newspapers. Please go away and do not scare me anymore. Understand?"

"Yes," Joel said. "I understand."

Ricky walked away with the newspapers to deliver. Every day, Ricky delivered newspapers to forty houses. He got paid one dime for each house. That meant he made four dollars every day for delivering newspapers.

Joel watched Ricky walk away to deliver newspapers.

Joel followed. But Joel stayed hidden from his older brother.

3

Soon, Joel saw Ricky pull out a slingshot from his other pocket.

Joel wanted to ask why Ricky needed a slingshot to deliver newspapers. But Joel stayed hidden from his older brother.

Then Joel saw why Ricky needed a slingshot.

When Ricky passed by a house with squirrels in a big tree, Ricky shot marbles from the slingshot at the squirrels.

It made the squirrels run away.

Ricky laughed at the squirrels.

Ricky did not see Joel come up from behind.

Joel tapped Ricky on the shoulder.

It scared Ricky.

Ricky jumped.

When Ricky landed, Joel asked him a question.

"Why are you mean to the squirrels?" Joel asked.

"What do you know?" Ricky asked. "You are only seven. And I told you I did not need your help to deliver the newspapers. Please go away and do not scare me anymore. Understand?"

"Yes," Joel said. "I understand."

Ricky walked away with the newspapers to deliver. Every day, Ricky delivered newspapers to forty houses. He got paid one dime for each house. That meant he made four dollars every day for delivering newspapers.

Joel watched Ricky walk away to deliver newspapers.

Joel followed. But Joel stayed hidden from his older brother.

4

At the next house, a big, lazy cat was asleep on the sidewalk.

Ricky walked up the sidewalk.

The cat did not wake up.

Ricky stepped on the cat's tail.

The cat meowed very loudly. It ran away very fast.

Ricky laughed at the cat.

Ricky did not see Joel come up from behind.

Joel tapped Ricky on the shoulder.

It scared Ricky.

Ricky jumped.

When Ricky landed, Joel asked him a question.

"Why are you mean to the cat?" Joel asked.

"What do you know?" Ricky asked. "You are only seven. And I told you I did not need your help to deliver the newspapers. Please go away

and do not scare me anymore. Understand?"

"Yes," Joel said, "I understand."

"No," Ricky said. "I do not think you understand. Because you still follow me."

5

Then Ricky had an idea. He knew how he could stop Joel from following him.

"Joel," Ricky said. "Would you like to have a lot of money?"

"I like to have fun," Joel said. "I like to be with you because you are my older brother."

"But if you had money, you could buy things," Ricky said. "You could buy toys and have them for yourself. Remember how much you liked your teddy bear? It was a nice toy. You could have many other toys, too, if you had money."

"Oh," Joel said.

"Let me tell you why I deliver newspapers," Ricky said. "It is because of mystery pennies."

"Mystery pennies?" Joel asked.

"Yes," Ricky said. "Mystery pennies. They are new and shiny. They grow in mailboxes. When you deliver a newspaper to the house, you put the newspaper in the mailbox and find a mystery penny that you get to keep."

This was a lie. Every day, Ricky delivered newspapers to forty houses. He got paid one dime for each house. That meant he made four dollars every day for delivering newspapers.

Joel did not know his older brother would lie to him.

"Mystery pennies," Joel said. "I like that!"

"Yes," Ricky said. "Tomorrow, I will let you deliver my newspapers for me. Tomorrow, you can have all those mystery pennies."

"Thank you," Joel said. "You are the nicest older brother in the world."

6

The next day, Ricky ran ahead to all of the houses. He ran fast because he did not have to carry newspapers. He put a shiny new penny in each mailbox.

Then Ricky ran back to find Joel.

He gave Joel the newspaper bag.

It was very, very heavy.

"Now you can go get the mystery pennies," Ricky said. "Put a newspaper in each mailbox. You will find a shiny new penny in each mailbox. I will wait for you at home."

"Thank you," Joel said. "You are the nicest

older brother in the world."

Joel did not know his older brother would lie to him.

So Joel began to deliver all the newspapers to all forty houses.

7

It took Joel a long time to deliver all the newspapers. It also made Joel very tired. But when Joel got home, he was happy. Joel had forty shiny new pennies.

The dogs were happy, because Joel did not squirt water at them from a water pistol.

The squirrels were happy, because Joel did not shoot marbles at them from a slingshot.

The cat was happy, because Joel did not step on its tail when it was asleep.

Ricky was happy, too.

Ricky did not have to deliver the

newspapers. Ricky did not have to worry about Joel following him.

Best of all, Ricky made much more money than Joel.

Ricky got paid one dime for each house. That meant he made four dollars every day for delivering newspapers. And Joel got only forty cents for all his hard work.

It was not fair, but Joel did not know.

He trusted his older brother, Ricky.

After that, every day, Ricky ran ahead and put shiny new pennies in the mailboxes.

After that, every day, Joel carried the heavy newspapers and put them in the mailboxes.

After that, every day, Joel collected the shiny new pennies for his work.

After that, every day, Ricky made a lot of money for doing very little work.

All because he had lied to his little brother about mystery pennies.

Ricky thought he was very smart. Then something happened.

8

It was Ricky's birthday.

Ricky began to open his presents.

Ricky's dad gave him a long box wrapped in blue paper. Ricky opened the long box wrapped in blue paper. His dad had given him a fishing rod.

"Thank you, Dad!" Ricky said. "I have always wanted a fishing rod."

Ricky's mom gave him a small box wrapped in red paper. Ricky opened the small box wrapped in red paper.

His mom had given him a watch.

"Thank you, Mom!" Ricky said. "I have always wanted a new watch."

Then Joel gave Ricky a present.

It was a medium-sized box. It was wrapped in green paper.

"What is this?" Ricky asked. Joel had never been able to buy him a present before. Joel was only seven.

"It is a present," Joel said. "Because you are the nicest big brother in the whole world."

Ricky opened the medium-sized box wrapped in green paper. Inside was a new baseball.

"Thank you, Joel!" Ricky said. "I have always wanted a new baseball. But where did you get the money to buy it?"

"Mystery pennies," Joel said.

"Yes," Ricky's mom said. "Yesterday, Joel made me take him to the store. He had a big jar filled with shiny new pennies. I do not

know where he got all those pennies. But he spent them all on your birthday present."

"Yes," Joel said. "Because you are the nicest big brother in the whole world."

9

Ricky did not feel like the nicest big brother in the whole world.

He felt like the meanest big brother in the whole world.

After that, every day, Ricky did not run ahead and put shiny new pennies in each mailbox.

After that, every day, Ricky did not give all the newspapers to Joel to deliver.

No.

After that, every day, Ricky ran ahead and put dimes in the mailboxes.

After that, every day, Ricky stayed with Joel and helped Joel deliver the newspapers. Ricky kept half of the dimes. He gave Joel the other half of the dimes.

When they delivered the newspapers, they did not squirt water at the dogs with a water pistol.

When they delivered the newspapers, they did not shoot marbles at the squirrels with a slingshot.

When they delivered the newspapers, they did not step on the cat's tail when it was asleep on the sidewalk.

The dogs were happy.

The squirrels were happy.

The cat was happy.

Joel was happy because his big brother let him help with the newspapers. Joel was happy because now he got dimes instead of pennies.

And Ricky was happy, too.

Because Ricky knew he had the nicest little brother in the whole world.

A Lesson About Fairness

In *Mystery Pennies,* Ricky lies to Joel and makes him do all the work.

Sometimes we lie to others because we are being selfish. When we are mean to others and they are nice to us, it makes us feel bad! We should treat others the way we want to be treated. We should make it up to those we have hurt, like Ricky did with Joel.

To Talk About

1. What does it mean to be selfish?
2. When you lie to someone, how does that make you feel?
3. What can you do to show God's love to others?

> *"Love each other like brothers and sisters.*
> *Give your brothers and sisters more honor*
> *than you want for yourselves."*
> *Romans 12:10*

Award-winning author Sigmund Brouwer inspires kids to love reading. From WATCH OUT FOR JOEL! to the ACCIDENTAL DETECTIVES series (full of stories about Joel's older brother, Ricky), Sigmund writes books that kids want to read again and again. Not only does he write cool books, Sigmund also holds writing camps and classes for more than ten thousand children each year!

You can read more about Sigmund, his books, and the Young Writer's Institute on his Web site, *www.coolreading.com*.